MY FIRST DAY IN KINDERGARTEN

By
Faridat A. Audu

Copyright © 2023
Faridat A. Audu

ISBN
978-1-963974-71-3
978-1-963974-72-0
978-1-963974-73-7

Dedicated To

All my twenty-one siblings across the globe with some of whom I had the honor of experiencing beautiful memories of my kindergarten years. Those memories remain precious till present!

&

Our late sister & brother

Kafayat Akanke Owolabi

Abdul Waheed Alani Owolabi

You are both always in our hearts!

Atai was a loving five-year-old boy who adored spending time with his family.

Atai had always wanted a baby brother or sister,
someone he could play with.
Mommy had already informed Atai that he will soon be
welcoming his baby brother, he seemed to be having fun
with his baby brother.

His baby brother had arrived into this world.
Daddy decided to name him Ayegba.
The arrival of his baby brother always makes
him happy. Daddy decided to name him
Ayegba. Meaning the WORRIOR from Igala
land in Nigeria, Africa.

Ayegba was a happy baby.
Just like Atai, he too, had
a curious nature.
Atai and Ayegba had
another thing in
common; they both had
a loving nature.

Atai loved spending time with Mommy and Daddy and baby brother. Atai finally felt like his family was complete.

He woke up every morning and ran over to his baby brother's crib, leaning in to see if he was awake.

When his baby brother would wake up, Atai would play with him all day.

Atai would often bring him his bottle, and help Mommy when she would be giving Ayegba a bath.

Atai loved doing things for Ayegba. He enjoyed doing little things for him. Ayegba, too, seemed to enjoy having Atai around.

B A

Mommy and Daddy had
told Atai that Ayegba was his
responsibility, and that he should
always look after his little brother. Atai
loved being the responsible older son.

Atai would hug him, kiss
him and place all his toys in
front of his baby brother
to play with.

One day, Mommy and Daddy called him to the dining room.
"Atai, remember you will be starting kindergarten tomorrow," said Daddy.
Atai frowned, "I don't want to go to school!" he exclaimed.

Mommy and Daddy noticed that Atai was clearly upset about going to school and not being able to spend all day with his family.

First Day of Kindergarten
Mommy had an idea. "How about you visiting your new school with me?"

"Why do I have to go?"
"Won't Ayegba and Grandma be lonely without me?"
Atai asked a lot of questions, which showed Mommy and Daddy that he was not ready to leave his baby brother.

"Atai, dear, there will be a lot of children
your age there. You can make more friends,"
said Grandma.

Mommy, Daddy, and Grandma tried several different ways to convince Atai that he will love his first day at kindergarten but nothing seemed to work.

Atai was sitting on the rug, his arms folded. He kept saying, "No, I am not leaving Ayegba."

Mommy sat down with him and finally
convinced him.
Mommy said, "Atai, how about you buy
your baby brother a small gift on our way
home from school?"
Atai quickly said, "A gift? For Ayegba? Mommy,
I would LOVE to give him a gift!"

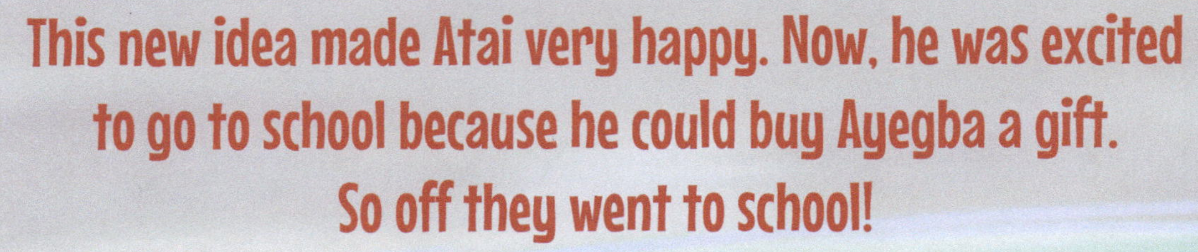

This new idea made Atai very happy. Now, he was excited
to go to school because he could buy Ayegba a gift.
So off they went to school!

When Atai entered, he saw that the school building was beautiful, colorful and there were a lot of kids there who looked very happy. Atai was still a little scared. He did not want to be left alone.

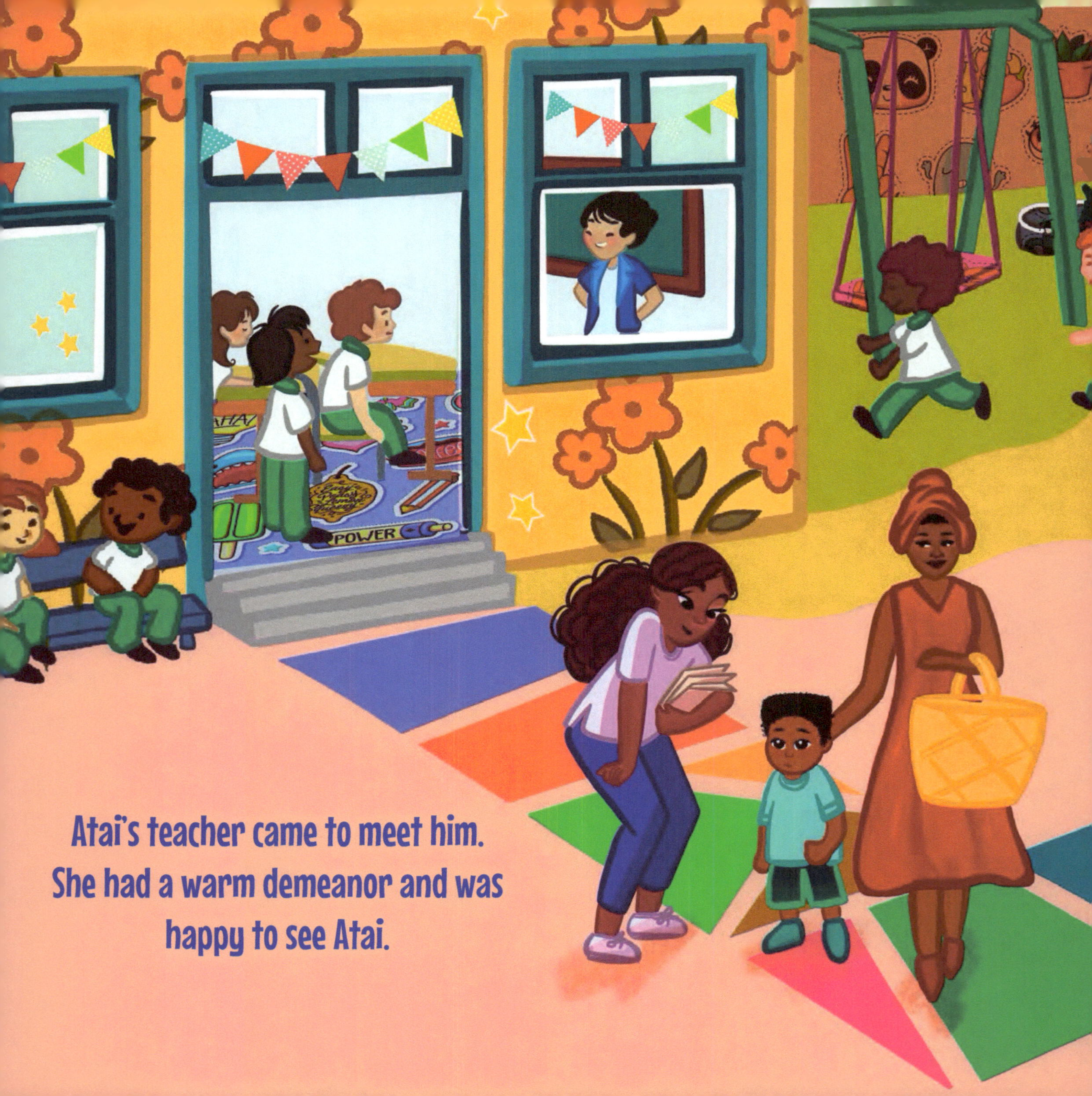

Atai's teacher came to meet him.
She had a warm demeanor and was
happy to see Atai.

Atai kept
holding on to
Mommy's hand.
His grip tightened, so
Mommy decided to walk into
the classroom with Atai.

Mommy knew that Atai would soon warm up to his teachers and fellow classmates.

When Atai walked into his classroom, he noticed it was full of interesting educational toys. All the children were happy and energetic.

Seeing this, Atai felt happy and quickly let go of his Mommy's hand. He gave his family goodbye kisses and gave his baby brother a kiss and a hug and then ran off to join his playmates.

hello
kinder
garten
FIRST DAY
SCHOOL
animals
plants
monsters
toys

Atai was brimming with excitement. Mommy was happy and relieved when she came to pick him up after school. She noticed how excited he was.

Atai kept telling Mommy about all the exciting things he did on his first day in school. "My first day in kindergarten was the best day ever, Mommy," said Atai.

"I'm glad to hear that, dear Atai," Mommy said, smiling.
Mommy then said, "Now, let's go to the toy store and choose a gift
for your brother."
"Wahoo! Let's gooo!" Atai exclaimed.

His first day at Kindergarten became a
memorable one!

The End.

Books in the
MY FIRST... Series:

My First Word

My First Day in Kindergarten

My First Lost Tooth

My First Snow Day

My First Sleepover

ABOUT THE AUTHOR

Faridat A. Audu is a Nigerian-Canadian early childhood educator with a Bachelor of Arts in English Language from Africa, a Professional Children's Writing Certificate from the USA, and a Master's degree in Educational Leadership from Canada. With an Award of Excellence in Early Childhood Education from Humber College and over 15 years of experience in the field, spanning Nigeria, Côte d'Ivoire, and Canada. Faridat is passionate about education and the founder of Global Vous Education INC., dedicated to fostering bilingualism and introducing contemporary educational trends with a focus on the Early Years and French language. Faridat is also the proud author of *My First Approach to Being Bilingual,* widely acclaimed for its invaluable guidance for English and French language learners.

Born in Lagos, Nigeria, Faridat has studied and traveled extensively worldwide. Currently, she resides in Ontario, Canada, with her husband and three sons. Her global perspective and dedication continue to inspire and empower educators, parents, and children alike.

ACTIVITY SECTION

Here are some fun activities that parents and educators could do with children. These activities would permit parents or educators to reflect on children's early years experiences in a fun, and interactive way.

(For Parents)
This activity is for parents. After reading "My First Day in Kindergatten" with your child, you can share with your children what their first day in Kindergatten was.

(For Educators)
This activity is for educators. As an educator, you can create classroom projects or exercises that would allow students to ask their parents about their first day in Kindergatten and share it with their peers the next day in class.

HAVE FUN!

9 781963 974720